Alexar
and the Gander

by Margaret Kirk   Illustrated by Martin Wright

© THE MEDICI SOCIETY LTD · LONDON · 1990   Printed in England. ISBN 0 85503 161 1

Alexander was six.

He lived with his parents in the old blacksmith's cottage which stood on the bend of the country road that ran through the village.

He was quite a good boy except for
one thing – he teased.

He teased
his dog,

he teased his cat,

he teased anything smaller than himself.

His mother got very cross with him.

'One day,' she said, when Alexander had been teasing the cat,
'you will have to pay for your teasing… you wait and see!'

Next to Alexander's house lived Uncle Fred. Uncle Fred's house was long and low with diamond-paned windows and blue curtains.

He had lots of animals and poultry. Cows, pigs, a horse and hens; but the creature that ruled the farmyard was Gander the goose.

Gander guarded the farm, keeping watch over his geese and goslings and letting Uncle Fred know when someone came to the door, by honking and hissing.

Gander loved to sit in the shade of the old forge at the side of Alexander's garden. The forge was no longer used for shoeing horses, but the anvil and bellows were still there beside the hearth.

One day Alexander went inside the forge and wandered around in the gloom looking for something to do. In one corner he found a long stick. 'Just the thing for poking about with,' he said to himself.

There was a loose brick in the wall near the floor. He pulled hard and the brick came away. He looked through the hole and saw Gander preening himself outside.

He poked the stick through the hole
and tickled Gander under his wing. Gander was furious.

He honked and hissed and looked round to see who was tormenting him.

'Ho! Ho! you silly bird,' called Alexander through the hole and tickled him once more.

Gander came over to the hole hissing loudly. 'One day I will catch you, Alexander, and you will be sorry,' Gander's eye seemed to say.

Alexander ran as quickly as he could back to the house.

'Whatever is the matter?' Mother said
when she saw his red face.
'Have you been teasing again?'

'No,' Alexander
replied.

But he knew Gander would not forget and he was frightened.
'I'll keep away from that old bird,' he thought.

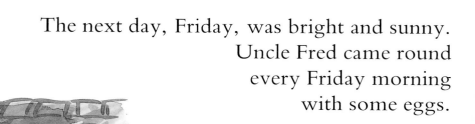

The next day, Friday, was bright and sunny. Uncle Fred came round every Friday morning with some eggs.

When he came Mother asked him if they could have a picnic in his field. 'I don't mind at all,' said Uncle Fred. 'Of course you can, and if I've time I'll come too.'

'But, young Alex, remember to close all the gates, we don't want the animals wandering through the village, do we?'
'No,' said Alexander.

11

Uncle Fred went back to feed the animals. Alexander saw him waving his walking stick at Gander. Gander was afraid of the walking stick.

Alexander went back indoors. He teased the cat with a piece of string.

'Alex, stop teasing the poor cat and help me carry out the picnic.'
Alexander jumped up and ran into the kitchen. Mother had a big tray on the table. On it stood three china mugs and two plates of sandwiches, covered with blue napkins. There was also a cake and a white jug filled with hot milky tea.

They carried out the tray and a rug and called on Uncle Fred to tell him the picnic was ready.

Uncle Fred came out wearing his sun hat and carrying his walking stick.
'I'll need this to frighten Gander off,' he said.

They had to cross over Gander's field to get to the picnic place.
'Last man shut the gate,' said Uncle Fred.
Alexander was feeling hot and lazy and his thoughts were on the picnic.

He could not be bothered to shut the gate.
He gave it a quick tug and left it standing half open.

They had their picnic under the tall trees in the hedgerow.

Afterwards Alexander wandered along the side of the field by the stream. He took off his boots and socks and paddled. He was having a wonderful time.

When he was tired of playing in the water, he lay down on his back in the long grass. Bees and butterflies flew above him and settled on the grasses and clovers that stood out tall against the blue sky.

The buzzing of the bees and the popping of the warm grass seed-heads made him feel drowsy.

He fell asleep.

The sound of his mother's voice
calling woke him up.

'Alexander, it's time to go back home! Where are you?'
Alexander stood up and waved. Uncle Fred and Mother were
already carrying the tray and empty plates back across the field.

'Bring the rug with you, please!' Mother called
when she saw him waving.

Alexander ran over to pick up the rug.
Just then he caught a movement from the corner of his eye.

Gander stood there staring at him with a wicked look on his face.
Mother and Uncle Fred were a long way away now.
Alexander's legs turned to jelly.

He couldn't move.

Gander hissed and spat and flapped his wings and stretched his neck towards him.

Gander moved forward, hissed again, and stretched out his neck once more.

He took Alexander by the seat of his pants and spun him round and round, holding him tightly in his beak.

Alexander was terrified.
'Help! Help!' he yelled.
He felt dizzy and sick.

Uncle Fred and Mother heard him call and
Uncle Fred ran back over the field
brandishing his stick.

Gander dropped Alexander and backed away hissing. He stalked off honking
indignantly back to his field.

Alexander was crying but not hurt.
He had had a nasty shock.

Uncle Fred picked him up.
'Oh, Uncle Fred!' sobbed Alexander,
    'I will never, never tease anything again.'

Uncle Fred looked at him.
'Gander has taught you a lesson,
Alexander,' he said.

'Alexander, what a fright you gave
us,' said his mother, 'but perhaps
it will teach you not to tease.'

Alexander looked down at the ground,
he felt very silly.
He was glad to be safely back
with Mother.

The next day he went to the forge and looked through the peep-hole.

Gander was there with his family, keeping watch as usual.

Alexander quietly picked the brick up from the floor and put it back in place.